LEGO®

JURASSIC WORLD

DINOSAUR DISASTER!

ADAPTED BY MEREDITH RUSU

FROM THE SCREENPLAY BY
JONATHAN CALLAN AND JIM KRIEG

SCHOLASTIC INC.

This is Claire. She's very smart. She's also very busy.

That's because she runs Jurassic World, a Park for dinosaurs! It's in the middle of a big green jungle.

Claire *loves* Jurassic World. It's her favorite place ever. She loves the Aviary, Main Street, and the control room, where she can see all the dinosaurs in the Park, like Echo, the Raptor. She loves big dinosaurs like the T. rex, and she really loves colorful dinosaurs.

Charlie

T. rex

Dilophosaurus

Echo

One day, at the Park, there's an accident.

Simon Masrani, the owner of Jurassic World, crashes his helicopter into a building where the flying dinosaurs live. After the crash, all the flying dinosaurs escape!

Without the flying dinosaurs, Jurassic World is short an attraction.

"Claire, you have to think of something to replace them," Simon tells her. "Otherwise, people will stop coming to Jurassic World. It's up to you to save the Park!"

IT'S UP TO YOU!

Claire is worried. "If only we had a super-cool new building," she says. "Or . . . a super-cool new *dinosaur*. That's it!"

Claire runs to tell her work friend Owen her idea. He's a dinosaur trainer at Jurassic World who has four trained Velociraptor friends.

"I know what our new attraction should be!"
Claire says excitedly. "A new dinosaur!"

But Owen shakes his head. "You can't just
build a dinosaur."

They go see Dr. Wu, the Jurassic World scientist.

It turns out, he can *totally* build a dinosaur! He's done it before!

NO PROBLEM!

Dr. Wu's science combines different dinosaurs together, into megadinosaurs! "This seems like a really bad idea," says Owen.

But Claire is happy. If Dr. Wu invents a brand-new dinosaur, lots of people will come to Jurassic World and the Park will be saved!

The next day, Claire meets with Owen.

"It took all night," she says. "But Dr. Wu has come up with the smartest, fastest, coolest dinosaur ever." She takes Owen up to a closed-off room that is above a pen, a big area with walls all around it.

Inside the pen below is a new dinosaur: the Indominus rex!

Owen is upset. "What does she do?" he asks.

"She is faster, larger, and smarter than any other dinosaur," Dr. Wu says. "She can also change colors. Watch this!"

He throws the Indominus rex a hot dog. When she eats it, she changes from purple to pink to plaid.

"Ooh! Plaid is a new one!" Claire says.

"Wait, she eats hot dogs?" asks Owen.

"Yes," says Claire. "We even have a guy in a hot dog costume feeding her. He throws hot dogs into the pen so the kids can watch her eat!"

"This is bad, Claire," Owen warns. "You can't give a dinosaur hot dogs. You'll spoil her!"

Claire shrugs. "I don't see the big deal about giving her hot dogs if she likes hot dogs. What could go wrong?"

Just then, something goes *very* wrong. The Indominus rex finishes all the hot dogs in her pen, but she's still hungry! That's when she spots the man in the hot dog costume . . .

UH . . .

The Indominus rex thinks the man *is* a hot dog! She breaks out of the pen and chases him! "Told you so," says Owen.

"Quick!" cries Claire. "We have to catch her!"

The guards run in with lassos and nets. But the Indominus rex is too strong. She breaks loose and runs into the jungle.

Luckily, the hot dog man is able to hide. "Whew," he says. "I need a raise."

Soon, it is nighttime. The guards have to find the Indominus rex in the dark.

Everyone hops into trucks and begins driving through the jungle.

Claire spots the missing dinosaur. "There," she yells. "The Indominus rex!"

They speed up, but Claire's truck goes too fast. It crashes, and Claire goes flying . . . right onto the Indominus rex's back!

"Claire, you have to jump!" Owen yells.

Claire takes a deep breath and slides down the Indominus rex's tail, just like a playground slide. Owen catches her. She's safe!

But the dinosaur is still on the loose.

"Our trucks can't keep up with her," says Owen. "It's time to do this dinosaur style."

He whistles to his trained Raptor friends, who have been following him. "Come on," he calls to them. "Corner that dinosaur! Come on, Blue! There you go, girl!"

The Raptors surround the Indominus rex. She grunts at them. The Raptors grunt back.

"Uh . . . what's she doing?" Claire asks.

Owen's eyes grow wide. "She's talking. That dinosaur must be part Raptor!"

The Indominus rex leads the Raptors away. They're going to take over the Park!

"We have to stop them before they form an entire dinosaur army," Claire says. "Owen, I have an idea. But for this to work, we need to move fast."

"What are you going to do?" he asks.
Claire smiles. "We're going to need a lot of hot dogs!"

Soon, Claire's plan is set. They've cooked every hot dog on the island and made a trail of them leading from the jungle back to the pen the Indominus rex escaped from. If she follows the trail, she'll fall back in!

Claire and Owen watch from a safe hiding place. The ground begins to shake . . .

It's the Indominus rex!
She eats the trail of hot dogs
one by one.

But just as she's about to eat
the last hot dog, she stops. Her
tummy rumbles.

"What's wrong?" Claire asks nervously.

"It's the one thing we never accounted for." Owen groans. "She's got a bellyache!"

The Indominus rex roars and begins breaking everything in sight! The Raptors join her. It's dinosaurs versus humans!

"Hold on!" Owen exclaims. "I'll be right back!"

Owen races away—he knows a secret place where a bunch of other new hybrid dinosaurs Dr. Wu created live.

Humans may not be able to stop the Indominus rex . . . but other dinosaurs can! "All right, you crazy creatures," he says. "Time to earn your lunch!"

Meanwhile, Claire faces off against the Raptors.

"I order you to stop and help us," she yells sternly. "Don't make me take away your vacation days!"

The Raptors gulp. They didn't even know they *had* vacation days! They move to help the guards. Now the Indominus rex is furious!

The mighty Indominus rex steps forward. The ground shakes. But this time, it's not her causing the tremors . . .

. . . it's Owen and all of Dr. Wu's other dinosaurs! They've come to save the day!

The other dinosaurs surround the Indominus rex. They push her back toward the pen and she falls right in!

"Hooray!" the friends cry. "We did it!"

"Thanks to your dinosaur-training skills," Claire tells Owen.

"And to your quick thinking," Owen adds. "I have to hand it to you, Claire. When Simon said to save the Park, I don't think he meant to save it from a giant new dinosaur."

Claire smiles. "But we sure did."